The Teazles' baby bunny

Written by Susan Bagnall

Illustrated by Tommaso Levente Tani

Published by
British Association for Adoption & Fostering (BAAF)
Saffron House
6–10 Kirby Street
London EC1N 8TS
www.baaf.org.uk

Charity registration
275689 (England and Wales) and SCO39337 (Scotland)

Reprinted 2010, 2011

British Library Cataloguing in Publication Data
A catalogue record for this book is available from the British Library

ISBN 978 1 905664 49 8

Project management by Shaila Shah, BAAF
Illustrations by Tommaso Levente Tani
Designed and typeset by Andrew Haig & Associates
Printed in Great Britain by the Lavenham Press
Trade distribution by Turnaround Publisher Services, Unit 3,
Olympia Trading Estate, Coburg Road, London N22 6TZ

Printed on FSC certified, chlorine-free paper

The author
Susan Bagnall lives in Scotland with her husband
and daughter. She is a qualified speech and language
therapist and is currently working as a playleader in a
pre-school group.

The illustrator
Tommaso Levente Tani (www.leventetani.com)
is a Tuscan picture book illustrator and author based
in London.

For Alice,
our own precious daughter

The Teazles lived in a bright, cosy burrow,

By a sycamore tree in Foxaway Hollow.

Their home was a happy one except for one thing...

They'd no baby bunny and the joy that would bring.

Mr McBadger knew of their plight,

And went to their house on a cool summer night.

'I've news of a baby, a bunny no less,

Who needs a new home and we think yours is best.'

The Teazles were speechless,

They danced round for joy.

At long last they'd have

Their own girl or boy.

They picked up the phone to tell all those they knew,

Of the happy event and the day baby was due.

All of their friends watched on with glee,

As they readied their home by the sycamore tree.

They made a pram from reeds, moss and wood,

With stones for the wheels, tied as tight as they could.

They made lots of toys, they put up a cot,

And painted a bedroom for their tiny tot.

With each day that passed their excitement grew,

They just couldn't wait to see each day through.

So they counted the days till McBadger came by,

With a wee bunny bundle held tight by his side.

welcome baby bunny

'This is your baby, to love as your own.

I know this will be a wonderful home.'

The Teazles cuddled their new baby bunny,

And said, 'We're your new daddy and mummy'.

And from that day on, by the sycamore tree,

The Teazles were happy as happy could be.

The End